Mittie Cuetara

Terrible Teresa

and Other Very Short Stories

Dutton Children's Books  New York

This is to Sam, for everything . . .

and

to Daniel boy, just for being your own sweet self

Library of Congress Cataloging-in-Publication Data

Cuetara, Mittie. Terrible Teresa and other very short stories / by Mittie Cuetara. — 1st ed.   p. cm. Summary:
A collection of four-line rhyming stories, including "Go Fish," "Baby Light-fingers," "The Sailor's Lament," and
"Outer Space."
ISBN 0-525-45768-2 (hc)   1. Children's stories, American.   [1. Stories in rhyme.   2. Short stories.] 1. Title.
PZ8.3.C88655Th 1997 [E]—dc21 96-29727 CIP AC

Published in the United States 1997 by Dutton Children's Books,
a division of Penguin Books USA Inc.
375 Hudson Street, New York, New York 10014

Designed by Semadar Megged
Printed in Hong Kong
First Edition
10 9 8 7 6 5 4 3 2 1

Contents

The Story of Fred

This is a boy named Fred.

He hates **to go to bed**.

He hides out in the shed

and stays awake instead.

5

The Dog Show

Oscar's dog is very fat.

Lisa's dog looks like a rat.

Jane's is an aristocrat.

Leon's dog is...oops, a cat!

Terrible Teresa

Did you make the baby wail?

Did you leave a sticky trail?

Did you pull the kitty's tail?

You must go to baby jail!

GO FISH

My fish was so friendly and kind

with a fine physique and an excellent mind.

I don't think he liked being confined.

He's gone off and left me behind.

the Nature of things

In early spring

things take wing —

some that sing

and some that sting.

Daby Light-fingers

We can't get very far.

We cannot start the car.

The keys are gone —oh, please

won't you tell us where they are?

13

A cowboy on his favorite horse

fell into the prickly gorse.

Some things he said were very coarse.

Later on, he felt remorse.

Queen of the Playground

First I go on the slide.

Then it's time for a ride.

Oops! We're going to collide.

This is a good place to hide.

A Very Friendly Cat

You can see the kitty there

underneath your dining chair.

He would like for you to share.

DON'T YOU DARE!

21

THE SAILOR'S LAMENT

Once I had a red sailboat.

I took it to the pond to float.

But when I ran to get my coat,
it was devoured by a goat!

WILD THING

Kitty stalks his prey,

dreams of a fillet.

Baby wants to play.

Kitty says, "No way!"

King of Beasts

The lion in the jungle roars.

He's happy chasing wild boars.

Then he does his evening chores.

And when he goes to sleep...he snores.

OUTER SPACE

Edie went to outer space.

She found a strange and different race.

Although it seemed a friendly place,

she brought her mommy, just in case.

Our Vacation

The view from the automobile...

Our campsite—so very ideal...

The two of us swimming with zeal...

The ants that made off with our meal...

THE END